SHANE SIMMONS

ISBN: 978-1-988954-06-6

Choke the Chicken
Copyright © 2016 by Shane Simmons
All Rights Reserved.

Published by Eyestrain Productions
eyestrainproductions.com

Originally published by Exile Editions in The Exile Book of New Canadian Noir, 2015.

T HE CARNIVAL, as it always did, as it always would, came to town. It was late in the spring, and the air was still cool. The snow was long gone, and the mud it left behind had had weeks to bake under the sun and transform into solid ground. Solid enough to pitch the tents that would house clowns and animal acts, and anchor the steel rides that would twirl and pitch and whip riders around with all sorts of nausea-inducing contortions. The setup was long and arduous, lasting days longer than it would cater to the public. When at last it opened its gates for business, the fair would spend a single weekend doing its very best to pick the pockets of everyone in town before packing up and moving to the next vacant field in its seasonal agenda.

Clive Whitworth had watched the tent peaks and the high rides slowly poke up over the town's modest skyline from his classroom window as the carnival was erected. The anticipation became unbearable as the weekdays dragged on, and Clive earned himself three separate detentions for ignoring his lessons in favour of gazing out the window. Such punishment had no effect on him or his carnival daydream. He only saw the extra half hours of after-school incarcerations as an opportunity to observe the distant construction from the slightly different vantage point offered by the windows of the detention room.

Although many of the other children in the school felt the same eager expectation for the weekend event, their interest was not aligned with Clive's. The enjoyment they derived from the attractions the annual carnival offered was more general, less focused. The fact was, Clive didn't particularly care for most of the spectacles that constituted a proper fairground. The rides made him sick, the candy floss gave him a belly ache. He didn't like clowns, and he cared even less for animals. What Clive liked was a challenge.

At long last, the school week dragged to its merciful end. It was late in the school year, and with the carnival in town, only a few of the most joyless teachers bothered to assign homework. None of them expected any of it to be done by Monday. In an otherwise dull town, this weekend would be a buzzing hive of entertainment options. No one would be wasting a single moment struggling through rudimentary algebra problems when there was so much fun to be had.

After a fitful night of sleep, Clive was up early. He could barely be convinced to finish his breakfast. Only the threat of withholding his allotment of fair money could keep him seated through his final bite of waffle and last strip of bacon. Once the go-ahead was finally issued by his parents, Clive threw on a light jacket and leapt from the front porch, dashing to the outskirts of town without ever stopping for breath or slowing his pace. He arrived at the wooden-placard gates of the carnival in eight minutes flat, beating his previous record by three. His growth spurt over the past year probably accounted for this, giving his legs an extra few inches of reach with each running stride.

The setup was nearly identical to the previous spring's and Clive remembered it well. Tickets for the rides and the shows could be purchased at a centrally located booth. Some shows cost one ticket, others two. The same went for the rides. The merry-go-round and the Ferris wheel, the tilt-a-whirl and the pirate ship, were all placed in their designated spots, spaced apart by the tents with the dancing dogs and the horse that could count. One strip along the border of the fairgrounds, stretching all the way from the funhouse to the haunted house, was where the carny booths were. Set in rows and forming an alleyway for games of chance and skill, they were ready to entrap anyone who dared navigate the gauntlet. Tickets wouldn't buy you a chance to win a stuffed toy here. Only cold hard cash could buy you a game. And the carnies would make sure you parted with a great deal of your cash before permitting you to walk away with a prize worth a fraction of what you spent to win it.

The lineup at the ticket booth was long and slow. Clive didn't care. He wasn't interested in tickets and didn't plan to purchase a single one. He was there for the games alley.

Clive considered himself a master of the games. He was undefeatable at the ring toss, always on target with a dart, air rifle or water pistol, and never failed to knock down a pyramid of cans with his three-ball allotment. Back home, stashed in a trunk in his closet, was his bounty from previous years. Plush pets, velvet posters, and plastic doohickeys of all sorts attested to his undeniable skill. He could have filled his entire room a dozen times over if his mother let him keep all the giant stuffed animals he'd won from the upper echelon of prizes. But they took up far too much space, and Clive had to admit they were garish, cheaply made, and filled with who-knows-what. One by one, he'd given them all up as they were pressed into service as gifts for birthdays and baby showers. He preferred to pore over his more compact collection of victories, often harder won. The prizes were all worthless junk, Clive was well aware, but to him they were more highly valued than mere money. They were testaments to his skill, well-honed through years of off-season practice.

Come carnival time, Clive would descend on the games alley and clean up. He would systematically travel from booth to booth, winning prizes, upgrading to bigger and better trophies, giving lesser ones away to friends who inevitably passed by on their way to the next ride or circus act. He wouldn't be satisfied until the carnies had all barred him from their individual booths for winning too much. That, to Clive, was the ultimate achievement, the one true prize he was really after. He'd made a clean sweep two years in a row now, banned for life from every single games booth. The lifetime ban was meaningless. The carnies never remembered him from year to year. They toured too many towns, saw too many faces. And Clive was still a growing boy. He hardly looked like the same kid who'd mopped the floor with them last year, or the year before.

Clive strolled the alley, checking out the games, watching the usual variety of unskilled marks lose their money as they missed their targets, failed to pop a balloon, or bounced a ball off the rim of what appeared to be an undersized non-regulation basketball hoop. The suckers. Clive had long ago figured out how all the games were rigged—how the odds were always stacked against the players like a crooked casino. He had also figured out how this gave him an unfair advantage, showing him the path to victory time and again. Practicing at home with some of his own roughly recreated challenges, he had vastly improved his skills, and had solved some of the trickiest deceits. The carnies always seemed to know how to win at their own games when they demonstrated to passersby how easy they were. Through observation and training, Clive had determined what sort of counter-intuitive backspin to give his ball throws, what sort of flick of the wrist could vastly improve his odds of landing a ring around a bottle neck, and where to aim an air rifle that had purposely had its sights miscalibrated.

The games were his to dominate. Clive's only question was where to begin.

"Are you smarter than The World's Smartest Chicken?"

This question was asked in bold red paint on an arched sign over a wheeled cart. On one side of the cart was a three-by-three grid of lights randomly flashing Xs and Os. On the other was a glass cage that held a disinterested-looking white chicken. The only other prominent feature on the cart was a coin slot, yawning open, eager to be fed. Clive had never seen anything like it before. Not at this fair, not anywhere. It was a confusing, alien addition to the landscape he'd memorized over the course of his gaming adventures.

One of the carnies selling three dart-throws at a wall of yellow, red and blue balloons observed Clive's long, thoughtful contemplation of the new attraction that had joined the alley this season. The carny was old, grizzled, a long-time veteran of the carnival and at least half a dozen just like it in years gone by. He knew a million ways to fleece the public out of the contents of their wallet, a dollar at a time if he could, a nickel at a time if he had to. But even in his advanced years, he was always open to learning a fresh approach. The World's Smartest Chicken was the latest trick up his sleeve. He'd been the loudest advocate for the chicken rig when one came on the market. It had been a tough sell to his fellow carnies, but none could denounce the benefit of a whole extra booth that didn't need to be manned by any additional employees and ran entirely on grain and a small amount of electricity. His argument won them over in the end and they all chipped in to buy it once they agreed to reap an equal share of its take.

The carny saw that curiosity had its hook in the boy.

"Give it a go, son. It won't bite," he encouraged. "Not tucked away behind that sheet of glass, it won't."

"How does it work?" Clive asked.

"It's tic-tac-toe. You know how tic-tac-toe works, don't ya?"

"Of course I do. But does the chicken?"

"Sure it does. Says it's The World's Smartest Chicken, don't it? You pop a dime in the machine and you play a game. If you beat it, well then, congratulations. If you tie it, then I guess you're only as smart as a chicken. And if you lose... Well, I wouldn't go telling anyone I'd lost a game of tic-tac-toe to a chicken, that's fer sure."

Clive's eyes fixed on the chicken behind the window. It didn't look any different from any other chicken he'd ever laid eyes on in his life. And out in his rural county, that amounted to a lot of chickens.

Almost unconsciously, Clive's hand slipped into his pants pocket and jingled the change nestled at the bottom. When he realized what he was doing, he removed his hand, only to find he'd come up with a single dime. This wasn't on his agenda, this uncharted attraction. Clive had a carefully calculated plan of attack. He knew which booths to hit first, which to hit last, and how long it would take him to work his way up to the top prize at each one. But this — this thing — stood in his way. There was no prize to be won, beyond the simple self-satisfaction of victory. Nevertheless, it stood as a barrier between him and his weekend loot. To ignore it, to circumvent it, would be to leave a challenge unanswered, and Clive wouldn't be able to return to school on Monday with his head held high if he had refused to meet it head-on.

He reached forward, slowly, deliberately, and pushed the dime into the coin slot. It rattled and clunked its way through the inner workings of the mechanism before landing in the coin bin at the bottom. The light board reset itself and the flashing Xs and Os vanished for the commencement of a new game. Inside the chicken's glass booth, a small trapdoor painted with the words "Thinking Booth" popped open on one of the walls. The chicken immediately rose to its feet, toddled over to the booth, and began pecking at the space hidden away behind the door. In response, a bold red X lit up on the board in the upper-left corner.

Clive saw that each square of the light board had a button so the human player could respond with his own move. He pushed the one next to the centre square, claiming it with a blue O.

Again the chicken pecked at its thinking-booth and another X appeared, this one in the bottom right. Clive countered with an O in the bottom left. The chicken knew enough to block him with an X in the upper right.

Only at this moment did Clive realize he'd made a rookie error. Even little kids playing tic-tac-toe with crayons on bits of scrap construction paper in kindergarten knew better. You always play the corners in tic-tac-toe. It's not a sure way to win, but it's the only sure way not to lose. He'd left the chicken with two possible winning moves, and he could only block one of them.

Reluctantly, Clive chose one of his two blocks. With only one available move to win, the chicken seized it. The line of red Xs flashed victoriously, informing Clive he had lost. To his shame, he'd figured that out two moves ago. The question was, how did the chicken know?

"Tough break, kid," said the carny, who barely mustered enough politeness to keep from laughing out loud. "But like I said, that's one smart chicken."

Clive didn't respond, merely fumed. There was no recourse for the embarrassment but to dig into his pocket for another dime. To prove a point, he ran through a second match, quickly this time, playing the corners like he knew he should have from the start. The chicken once again played flawlessly, but with Clive responding to each move correctly this time, the game finished in a mathematically certain tie. Clive wasn't able to defeat the chicken, but at least he'd proved he could hold it to a draw—world's smartest or not.

Clive turned back to the carny, prepared to flash him a cocky grin. But the carny had already turned his attention to another mark—a teenage boy with a girl at his side he was eager to impress. There might have been as much as ten dollars to be made off him before the teen won a fifty-cent teddy bear to gift to the girl. That was much more pressing business than goading some kid into losing a couple of dimes to a chicken.

With no more audience to prove himself to, Clive nearly took the opportunity to walk away and get on with his day. But one nagging question picked at his ego. He'd battled The World's Smartest Chicken to a draw, but could he defeat it? Against his better judgment, Clive dug for a third dime to feed into the coin slot.

And so the day went, slipping away minute by minute until the minutes accumulated into hours. Clive stood there as the sun crawled across the sky and the shadows grew long, pumping nickels and dimes into the coin slot, matching wits with a chicken and coming up short each time. Dissatisfied with tie after tie, Clive attempted a variety of strategies to unnerve the chicken and throw it off its game. He tried any number of nonsense moves in order to confuse and bamboozle his opponent. Each ploy to lull the chicken into a false sense of security failed, every attempt to lure it into a trap was evaded. The chicken displayed nerves of steel and kept to its purely logical game plan. The more outrageous and unpredictable Clive tried to be on the game board, the more losses he managed to rack up, until his tie-loss ratio versus his chicken nemesis started to become very embarrassing indeed. Not until many years later, when Kasparov matched wits with Deep Blue, did two such divergent masters butt heads so spectacularly.

The comparison was apt, for it was not a flesh-and-blood chicken Clive sought to defeat, but a machine — a machine built to do two things and two things only. Deceive and eat coins. The role Clive had unwittingly volunteered for was the dupe in a magic trick — a magic trick so simple, you didn't need a magician to perform it — just a rudimentary computer program and a hungry chicken. Each time it was the chicken's turn to move and the "Thinking Booth" swung open, the bird would quickly step over to peck at its unseen control panel, as though it were selecting which square it wanted to fill next. In fact, the only thing on the chicken's tiny mind was food. Conditioning had taught it that pecking at the inside of the booth would, at least once per match, open the grain dispenser in the cage, offering a rewarding snack. The truth was that no chicken, even The World's Smartest Chicken, could wrap its head around the complexities of tic-tac-toe. It just wasn't their thing. The humans outside the glass prison might as well be feeding spare change into a toll booth for all the chicken knew or cared. Any perceived human-chicken interaction was entirely one-sided.

Nevertheless, it was a good life as far as chickens are concerned, or at least better than most could look forward to. The cage was reasonably spacious, the food, though intermittent, was plentiful. And as an added bonus, the chicken got to humiliate humans by the dozen daily, which it might have appreciated had it a clue. On this particular day, however, there was only one obsessive human to humiliate. Clive hogged the machine until closing, only pausing for brief trips to the Port-A-Potties and to break his modest wad of saved dollars for more dimes and nickels at the hotdog kiosk.

When the announcement came over the PA speakers that the carnival was now closed for the day and customers needed to clear the grounds, Clive was dismayed to find he'd gone through his entire bankroll without a single win to his name.

Back home, Clive picked at his dinner, hardly eating anything, not really hungry anyway. When asked if he had fun at the carnival that day, he mumbled something grumpy and indistinct and then excused himself for an early bedtime.

After dark, once the rest of the house was asleep, Clive made the rounds. There remained another whole day to bounce back and salvage the season, but he needed to replenish his ammunition. Silently he raided his father's bill fold, his mother's change purse, and his little sister's penny jar. He knew the theft would not go undiscovered for long, but the consequences were something he'd only concern himself with come Monday morning, once the carnival was gone from town and out of his reach for another year. Until that moment, Clive's only thought was fixed on saving face, defeating the chicken once and for all, and moving forward with his original agenda to crush all the other games in the alley. There was still time if he moved quickly. A good night's sleep and a fresh start with a fresh perspective was all he needed. He'd come at the chicken hard in the first few minutes of the Sunday opening, catch it unawares before it had a chance to get up to speed, and then move on to a more deserving challenge.

Clive was absent at breakfast the next morning. It was the only way to be sure he was first through the gate the moment the carnival reopened for the day. He was at the chicken stand moments later, before any of the carnies had even assumed their positions in their game booths. He had to wait an additional ten minutes until someone came around to plug the cart into an extension that ran to one of the fairground's generators. Clive killed the time by staring coldly at his opponent, trying to rattle the chicken as it stared back with one profiled eye.

Once power was restored, Clive was lightning quick with his first coin. His money from the day before had all been removed overnight, and he could hear his first dime rolling on its rim once it dropped into the empty change bucket inside the machine. He was five dimes into the rematch before anyone else stepped foot in the arcade strip to man the booths or try their hand at the games. Clive played fast and decisively, hoping a sudden rapid assault of matches would afford him the advantage. Once again, Clive's strategy proved futile. A night's sleep had not improved his performance, and an early start had not thrown the chicken off its game.

After his late-night thievery, Clive had started day two with even more cash in his pockets. He went through it all twice as fast as he had previously and was bankrupt by noon. He spent the rest of the afternoon wandering the fairgrounds, hitting up any school friends he could find for spare change. He was able to borrow a few coins here and there. Close friends were willing to advance him as much as a dollar at a time. All of it was fed to the chicken in short order. Still hours away from the carnival calling it quits for the weekend, Clive was destitute. Word of his desperate fundraising had spread and no more loans were forthcoming. Even old pals turned their backs on him and hid, ducking behind thick queues of people, or losing themselves in the Hall of Mirrors, rather than get tapped by Clive again.

Any other year, even short on cash, Clive would have lingered and watched the rides and listened to the screams and laughter. But there was no joy left in it. He couldn't even bring himself to return one final time to the games in order to watch the unskilled lose their money at challenges he himself had mastered. Not with that damn superior chicken standing there, looking down on him from inside its glass box, all-seeing and all-knowing—at least in regards to anything tic-tac-toe related. Clive instead decided that it was time to return home, have something to eat at last, and face the consequences of his crime if it had been found out.

"Where were you this morning?" his mother wanted to know. When Clive didn't come down for breakfast, she had been every bit as worried as doting motherhood required her to be. But she had guessed exactly where her son was—the only place he could be—and had not called around or made inquiries of the neighbours.

"I wanted to get an early start," Clive shrugged.

"There's money missing. Do you know where it is?"

"Yeah," admitted Clive, and braced for the third degree, the disappointment, the punishment.

Sent to bed without supper, grounded for weeks' worth of home detention, Clive felt the sting of defeat weigh on him more heavily than any loss he'd ever experienced in his softball league or at a spelling bee. This was a loss that mattered, that haunted him. Sleep would not come, and he felt certain a peaceful slumber would never be his again until he purged this loss from his troubled mind. Slipping out of bed after the rest of the house was down for the night, pulling his clothes back on, Clive knew the hour was very late, but there was still time to catch the carnival before it skipped town. There he would have to face the chicken one final time.

Clive was not stupid so much as stubborn. He couldn't let things lie, not where they were. Winning was no longer on his mind. The sole focus of his every thought now was revenge. It would be quick and easy as killings went. He could picture his hands around the chicken's throat, squeezing tight, choking off its air supply, crushing bones, snapping its arrogant neck.

Would his midnight act of murder be investigated, traced back to him? Would charges be laid, prison time served? It was, after all, only a chicken. But this was The World's Smartest Chicken. Surely there would be a reckoning for such a special animal. Clive supposed it would depend on just how brilliant the chicken was — if tic-tac-toe was its sole talent, or if it offered more to the world. It had been undeniably brilliant anticipating Clive's every move so far. Did the chicken foresee this one as well? Would it raise an alarm, clucking and screeching for salvation before Clive could sneak up on it and commit the deed? Clive considered all this, but recognized he'd spent the better part of two days second guessing himself into this position. Best now to simply act, swiftly and brutally and with a violence no chicken could hope to match.

When he arrived at the fairgrounds, the tents were already flat on the ground and folded up. The staff was hard at work, tearing down all the temporary structures and packing the clapboards and canvas away in trailers that would be hitched to trucks and rolled to the next town in a matter of hours. The rides were still standing, steel skeletons, dark and imposing by moonlight. The power was out, the cables were being collected and spooled, and it was too dangerous to dismantle the big attractions in the dark. They wouldn't be torn down until morning, once all the lighter, more basic elements were out of the way and on the road.

The carnival workers toiled by flashlight and bat-tery-operated lanterns. There was ample illumination for them to see what they were doing, but it was easy for one boy to slip by them unseen if he kept to the shadows. Clive's memory of the carnival layout helped him find his way in the dark without tripping over anything and calling attention to himself. It was a simple matter to find the games alley. The booths were empty now. Without their colourful prizes, blinking lights, bottles or balloons, they looked uniformly non-descript. The only stand in the strip that remained unique was the chicken's cart. The silhouette of its wagon-wheel spokes and the transparent glass cage stood out in the dim light that filtered through the grounds from the opposite end of the fair.

Clive could see the chicken sitting inside its cage, unaware of his presence. He approached the cart, look-ing for a latch that would open the glass box and allow him access to his enemy—a clear path to a neck that needed wringing. He ran his fingers around the frame, feeling for the mechanism, but found nothing. It was too dark to see how the box was opened. Clive consid-ered shattering one of the panes, ramming his elbow through it, hoping not to cut himself too severely. But that would alert the workers, rouse the chicken, re-move the advantage of surprise. He tried to calculate whether or not he would have enough time to get his fingers around the throat of a panicked and alarmed chicken before rescue was at hand.

Clive was still considering his options when he felt something underfoot. It was an extension cord. He reached down and hooked it with a couple of his fingers. Following it along its path, he arrived at a multi-socketed plug that rested at the end of a larger power line near one of the empty booths. Perhaps he could risk a little light to find his way in the dark, thought Clive. It might go unquestioned by the busy men long enough for him to accomplish the assassination and slip away unnoticed.

Clive plugged in the chicken cart and the tic-tac-toe board lit up. Reset, the game blinked twice and then defaulted into automatic mode. No one was feeding change into the coin slot, but tic was matched against tac in a brutal duel that ended in stalemate each time. Clive could see that it wasn't the chicken playing at all. The machine was playing itself. And there was something else he noticed by the light provided by the red and blue Xs and Os.

The chicken was brown.

"Who's that?" said a gravelly voice from behind one row of wooden stands. It was the old carny from the dart-toss—the one who had baited Clive into challenging the genius chicken. Clive's first instinct, having been discovered trespassing, was to flee. He fought the impulse, determined to seek answers instead.

Clive walked around the left flank of the games alley to address the carny directly. There was a small campfire burning behind the stands, with several wooden crates pulled up next to it. The carny was seated on one, warming himself over the modest blaze that had been invisible from the alley.

"What happened to The World's Smartest Chicken?" asked Clive.

The carny pointed at the chicken in the rig through a narrow gap in the alley's wooden façade. It remained nestled, eyes closed, dozing for the night.

"You're looking at it, kid."

"That's not the same chicken as before."

The carny considered the chicken currently residing in the glass cage, then returned his attention to the spit that was set up over the camp fire. He'd been cooking up some fowl for his dinner before the boy interrupted.

"No, I guess that makes this one the new world-champ."

"I don't get it? Did it beat the other chicken in a match or something?"

"You could say that," nodded the carny, tearing away a strip of greasy skin from the roasted bird's plucked breast as it sizzled over the open flame. "It wasn't no tic-tac-toe match, though. It was more of a taste test."

The carny cackled slightly to himself as he popped the loose skin into his mouth and sucked at the tips of his fingers where he'd just been holding it.

Clive noticed a small pile of discarded white feathers behind the games-alley backdrop. A slight nighttime breeze played with them, scattered them in random directions. They'd all be blown away by tomorrow, gone like the rest of the carnival.

"You want a drumstick?" asked the carny, tearing one of the tender legs off his meal and offering it to the boy.

Clive remembered the stories he'd heard of tribes in the deepest darkest jungles of the world. Some of them would eat their defeated enemies as a way to imbue themselves with their strength, their power. It was both a sign of respect for their fallen foes, and a way of stealing all they ever were and making it their own. Clive had thought that sounded kind of dumb when he first heard about it. But the way he saw things and the way he thought about them kept changing the more living he got under his belt. These days he wasn't so sure about much of anything. He wasn't even sure if that much uncertainty in life frightened or excited him.

"Yeah," he said, and sat down to eat.

About the Author

Shane Simmons is an award-winning screenwriter and graphic novelist whose work has appeared in international film festivals, museums and lectures about design and structure. His art has been discussed in multiple books and academic journals about sequential storytelling, and his short stories have been printed in critically praised anthologies of history, crime and horror. He lives in Montreal with his wife and too many cats.

Also by Shane Simmons

Novels

Necropolis
Sex Tape
Filmography

Booklets

Hot Pennies
Carrion Luggage
The Red Baron: An Ace for the Ages

Graphic Novels

The Long and Unlearned Life of Roland Gethers
The Failed Promise of Bradley Gethers
The Inauspicious Adventures of Filson Gethers

Last Words

Small-press publishers rely on reviews from readers like you to help get the word out about their books. Whether it's a simple star rating or a written critique, every bit of feedback helps convince the impersonal computer algorithms of Amazon, and other literary outlets, that the book you just read has merit and deserves more exposure. Please support independent authors, editors and publishers by taking a few moments to share your thoughts and opinions with other potential readers who may be sitting on the fence about trying an intriguing novel or collection. Your suggestions or comments can make all the difference when it comes to helping them find a new writer they'll like, or matching a struggling author with the readership he or she deserves. Thank you.